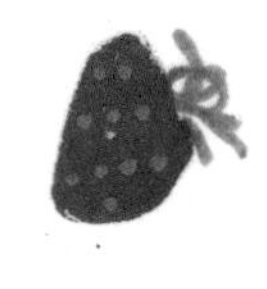

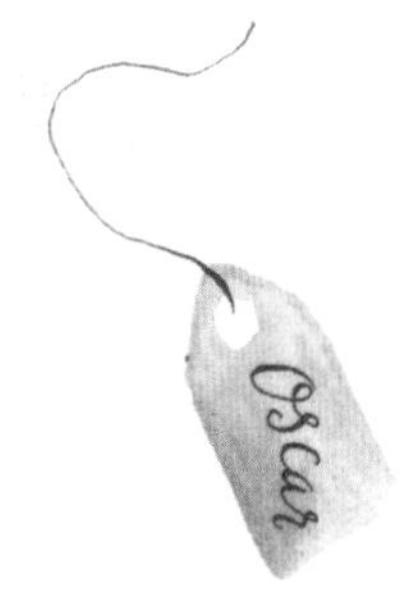

for azia, oscar, india & grace

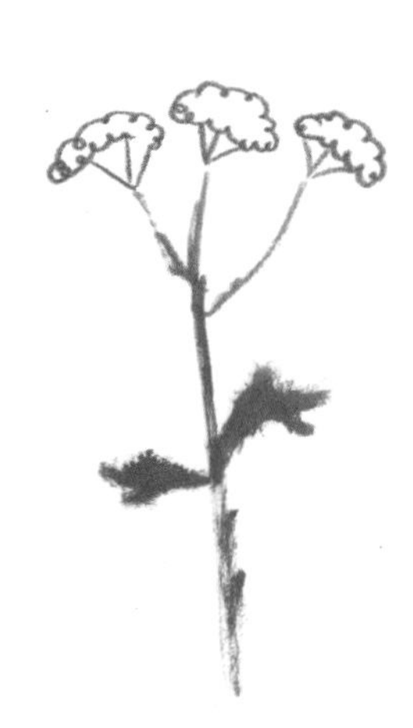

Published by Pucci Books Ltd on behalf of
Maggie and Rose in 2008

Maggie and Rose Ltd
58 Pembroke Road
Kensington
London W8 6NX

Pucci Books Ltd
32 Great Sutton Street
Clerkenwell
London EC1V 0NB

A CIP catalogue record of this book is available
from the British Library.

ISBN 978-0-9559352-5-1

Printed in Portugal

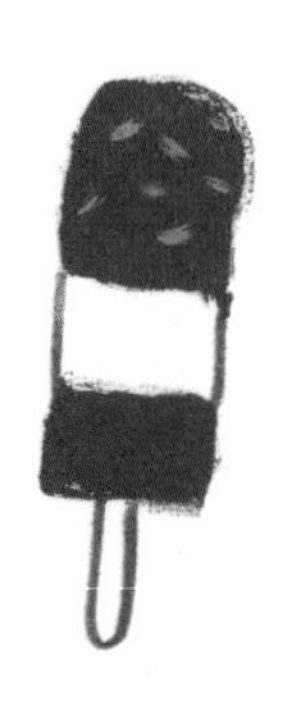

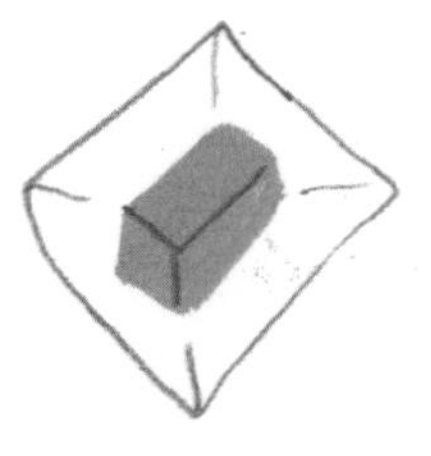

maggie rose oscar & bentley

oscar & bentley

totally save the day & are heros

by

mr z

These are just two girls. They're both pretty dumb.

This is my secret club but those girls keep getting in, which is really annoying.

This is me! I am a superhero called Oscar. I can do all sorts of super things like flying. I live off ice creams which I eat 3 at a time. I was sick once but don't ask me why. This is my dog Bentley. He is VERY fierce.

This is inside my Secret club. The girls have got in and are doing some pretty dumb things. Maggie, the one in the Spots, is making a cake which will probably be rubbish,

and Rose is putting some weeds
in a bucket, don't ask me why. I'm going to
do a painting. We're waiting
for a visitor from America.
I think he's my uncle, anyway
he's called uncle Fabiola and he
always brings us
AMAZING presents...

....One time he brought us a baby fire-breathing dragon but the Police took him away, don't ask me why, he was a lovely dragon.

Another time he brought us Mexican Jumping beans, you held on to them and you could jump REALLY high. My mum took that away, to play with it herself I suppose.

Just like I said it would Maggie's cake turned out rubbish,

and to make her
feel better
Rose covered the room
in
cream.

I decided
to do a
painting
of Bentley, Uncle
Fabiola loves paintings
of fierce dogs.

Rat-a-tat-tat-tat! Uncle Fabiola is very good at knocking.

'Howdy Oscar' he said, 'boy am I pleased to see you.' He said he was pleased to see Maggie and Rose too, but I think he was only pretending. The presents he brought were a pretty odd shape, I couldn't work out what they were by just looking

oscar

Rose x
Oscar x
Maggie x
Cake looks better

So we opened them.

Uncle Fabiola was smiling

as I ripped the paper off.

He has VERY bright teeth.

And what were the presents ?........

maggie x

.... scooters! oh dear,
we already had scooters,
but we pretended to be pleased
so not to hurt his feelings.
Then he **told** us they were actually
MAGIC SCOOTERS that could FLY.

Then I didn't have to pretend to be pleased any more because I **WAS**! And then he said 'Kiddoes they don't work on Sundays and don't ask me why, they just **DON'T** so remember it!'

But today was Saturday so it didn't matter.

I was just on my way outside to try it out when those girls made me come back and eat their stupid old cake. It was pretty horrible, but I ate five slices so as not to hurt their feelings.

oh crumbs

At last we
got outside,
me first!.....

.....I was about to press the magic button when I nearly crashed into a herd of dogs taking an old lady for a walk. She was quite upset because she had lost one, I didn't think it mattered as she had SO many. She said it DID matter but all I wanted was to go flying.

HooRAY! I pressed my magic button and me and Bentley flew up into the sky. I was very good at flying, much better than those girls. I did some loop the loops and gave some silly pigeons a fright.

It was brilliant fun, we flew all
over the roofs and chimneys
, from the London Eye to Trafalgar Square

where we saw Nelson standing
on a column. I made loads of
faces at him but he
didn't even smile.

Then it got dark which
was brilliant as it meant
that I could go and check
if the moon really is made
of cheese. but Rose said
NO! quite loudly. We had
forgotten to look for the
lost dog so we had to go
and Say Sorry to the
old Lady.

Bentley and me could smell sausages so we landed by them and THERE was the Old Lady. She had found her dog herself and was quite happy about it. Bentley asked the sausage man for a sausage when suddenly....

..... the Lady's hat blew off her head and got stuck on the hands of Big Ben.
'Oh no!' she said 'that was my best hat in the world, who will rescue it for me?'

BONG!

BONG!

NG!

BONG!

BONG!

This was a job for Superheros Oscar and Bentley. So we leapt onto our scooter and flew off to the rescue. I steered right up to the clock and then Bentley stuck out his paw and grabbed the hat just as the clock started bonging for midnight. It was VERY loud. And then the scooter stopped working, don't ask me why, and we floated down to the ground like a bag of chips.

real diamonds
The Old Lady was very happy, and she said that me
and Bentley were superheros, better than Batman and
Spiderman put together. Then she told us that she was
the QUEEN like on the stamps and money and we could
go back to her palace for a midnight feast.
we all went there on our scooters but she
took a taxi.

For the midnight feast we had chocolate eclairs and strawberry tarts and jelly AND sausages, so Bentley was happy too.

But the best thing was that Uncle Fabiola was there and he gave us all sunglasses so he could smile as much as he wanted and it wouldn't hurt our eyes.
z z z z

z z z z

bed

time

the

end

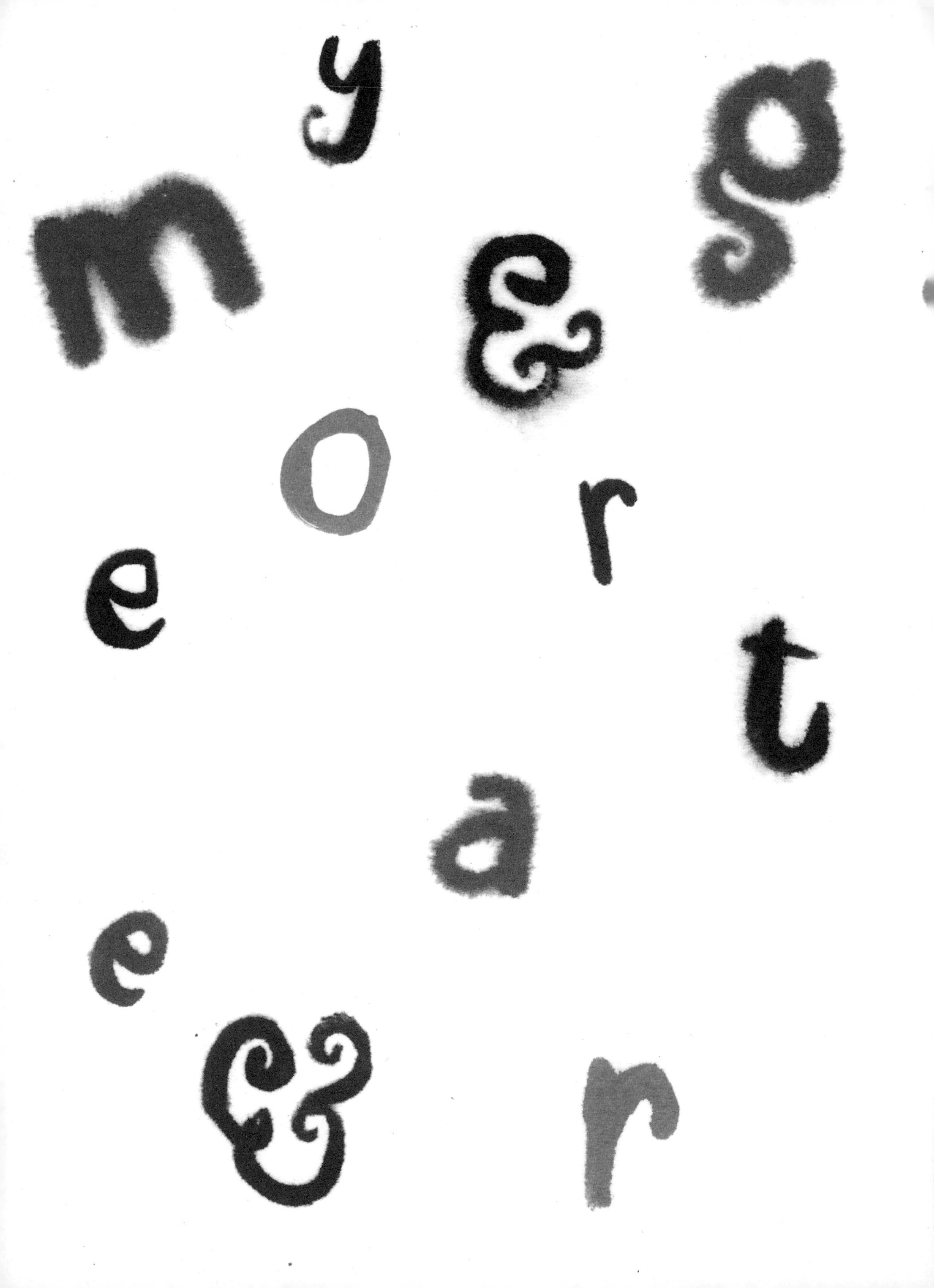